ROSY COLE'S
Worst~~Ever,~~
Best Yet
Tour of
New York City

ROSY COLE'S
Worst ~~Ever~~, Best Yet
Tour of
New York City

Sheila Greenwald

Melanie Kroupa Books
Farrar, Straus and Giroux
New York

For Melanie Kroupa and

Harriet Wasserman . . . who started

it all . . . again

Text and pictures copyright © 2003 by Sheila Greenwald
All rights reserved
Distributed in Canada by Douglas & McIntyre Ltd.
Printed in the United States of America
Designed by Jennifer Crilly
First edition, 2003
1   3   5   7   9   10   8   6   4   2

Library of Congress Cataloging-in-Publication Data
Greenwald, Sheila.
   Rosy Cole's worst ever, best yet tour of New York City / by
Sheila Greenwald.— 1st ed.
      p.   cm.
   Summary: Rosy plans to show her small-town cousin all the
amazing sights that make New York City such a great place to
live, but things do not go as she had hoped.
   ISBN 0-374-36349-8
   [1. Cousins—Fiction.   2. Family life—New York (State)—
New York—Fiction.   3. New York (N.Y.)—Fiction.]   I. Title.

PZ7.G852Rp 2003
[Fic]—dc21

                                                      2002192526

Contents

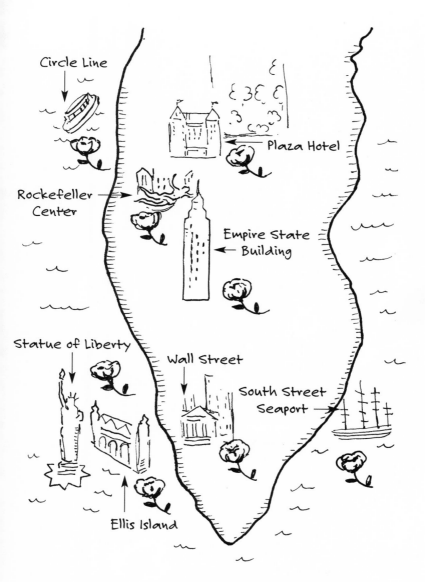

Circle Line

Plaza Hotel

Rockefeller Center

Empire State Building

Statue of Liberty

Wall Street

South Street Seaport

Ellis Island

ROSY COLE'S FABULOUS BIG ROSY
TOUR OF NEW YORK CITY

Sunday morning I was half asleep when my mother ran into my room. "Rosy?" she cried. "Your cousin Duncan is gone."

3

"Gone? Where?"

"His suitcase is gone, too." My mother stood over my bed. She looked terrible.

My father came up behind her. "He left a note," he said, holding the note in front of my face.

I sat up in bed and tried to read Duncan's handwriting.

Dear Aunt Sue and Uncle Mike,
  I'm sorry if I'm causing Trouble, but I can't go home Today—too many Things I never got To do. Please explain to my mom and dad.
  Thanks for letting me visit.
  I will be in Touch.
  If you really want To find me, Rosy will know where to Look.
              Sincerely,
              Your nephew
              D. Cole, Real New Yorker
P.S. Don't worry! ☺

"Do you know about this?" my mother asked.

My mouth was so dry I couldn't speak.

Over my head I heard my mother say to my father, "We never should have invited him. He was too young. What on earth will we tell his parents?"

Dad sat on my bed and put his arms around me. "Duncan thinks you can find him, Rosy," he said.

I shook my head. My teeth were chattering so hard that I still couldn't say a word.

Dad hugged me and said, "Please try to calm down, sweetheart. While Mom phones the police, try to think of what might have happened to your cousin Duncan . . ."

If this was a nightmare, I prayed I

would wake up. "I don't know where to begin," I sobbed.

"Why not at the beginning?" my dad suggested . . .

The Beginning.

Two weeks before Christmas, my mother opened the card on top of our pile of mail and held it out to Dad. "Holiday greetings from your brother, Grover," she said.

We all examined the photo on the front of the card.

And then we read the message.

Dear Mike and family,

Our one sorrow this time of year is that we live so far from family that Duncan is growing up without knowing his cousins. So here's an IDEA!

Duncan's school vacation falls during the same week our house is being plastered and painted. Dunky is timid about cities—but we thought he might prefer the soot, smog, and coughing crowds of your big city to the dust and paint fumes at home!

Could he come visit? He's a shy, quiet, stay-at-home kind of guy and wouldn't be any trouble.

Wishing you all the best this holiday season.

Emily, Grover, and Duncan

I began to jump up and down with excitement. "It's my vacation, too," I cried, holding up my calendar.

"But it isn't ours," Mom said.

"That doesn't matter," I insisted. "I'll take care of Duncan on my own."

"A week can be a long time if you don't hit it off." Dad sounded dubious. "Why don't you think about it?"

"I just did," I told him. "It's a definite date."

My name is Rosy Cole. I have two older sisters named Anitra and Pippa, a mother and father named Sue and Mike, and an Uncle Grover who is my father's brother. Fifteen years ago Grover married Aunt Emily and brought her to New York to meet our family. She said she liked us fine, but that our city was noisy and dirty; with so many people crowded together, it gave her "the willies" and she *never* wanted to come back. She never did.

AUNT EMILY IN NEW YORK

When I was four years old, our family made a trip to visit Emily and Grover. Mom said all the streets looked alike, and all the houses on the streets looked alike, and all the people in the houses looked alike, and, though she loved Emily and Grover, their place was so clean and empty it gave her "the willies" and she *never* wanted to go back. And we never did.

MOM AT UNCLE GROVER'S

Even though Duncan is my age, I don't remember him very well. Pippa and Anitra said he was shy.

Since he is shy, I sat right down to write him a note of welcome. I wanted him to know there were a LOT more interesting things to do than just "stay-at-home" at our place. To give him an idea, instead of using my usual stationery, I chose a card with the Statue of Liberty on it from my book of New York postcards.

Dear Duncan
Here's Lady Liberty.
She is just one of the "only in New York" landmark sites we'll visit on our Tour.
Can't wait to see you.
Your cousin
Rosy

When I showed my family the card at dinner, my sister Anitra frowned.

"Are you certain about this, Rosy?" she asked me. "You've only met Duncan once, when you were both four years old."

"He's a small-town boy whose parents don't like *any* city—especially New York," Pippa added. "He probably shares their feelings."

I shook my head. "Don't worry about that," I said. "I'm going to show Duncan Cole such an amazing time, he'll never be the same."

What I didn't know was, neither would I.

2

"I have this dreamy-looking cousin who is coming to stay with us over February vacation," I boasted to my friends Hermione and Christy as we walked to school the next morning.

"How come you never mentioned him before?" Hermione asked. She has a very suspicious nature.

"Because he lives on the other side of the country and they never visit."

"Do you have a picture?" Christy prodded. She's a model and very interested in photos.

I was ready. I took the card out of my pocket.

"He's dreamy all right," Christy said. "This picture is so bad the only way you'd know how he looked would be in your dreams." She handed the card back to me. "Mystery Boy."

"Mystery Boy?" Hermione grabbed the card, her face pink with excitement. "Let me see that."

I go to Miss Read's School, which is all girls and private. Sometimes my friends and I try to imagine the boyfriend of our dreams. Mine looks a little like Christy's brother Donald. Christy's dream boyfriend is in his last year of high school and super brainy. But Hermione's dream boyfriend is a mysterious stranger from a distant place.

"It's not easy having a guest all to yourself for one entire week," Hermione said. "Why not introduce Duncan to your classmates?"

"Because I invited Duncan Cole to show him New York, not to find him a girlfriend," I said, staring straight at Hermione. She pinched her lips together and frowned.

"But it takes a lot of preparation to show someone around all on your own," Christy warned. "When I visited my aunt and uncle in San Francisco, they made a tour kit for me, full of interesting things that would help me get to know the city. Every single day

16

they had a plan to take me someplace really special."

"Now, *that's* a good idea," I said while Hermione glared.

As soon as I returned home from school, I found a shoe box and got busy. It turned out I didn't need to buy a thing.

Then I sat down to make a plan. I wasn't going to take Duncan on a crammed double-decker bus full of sightseers while someone with a megaphone told us to look at this and that. Instead, I'd give Duncan The One and Only Personal and Individual Rosy Cole Tour of New York. I'd take him to visit every site in my book of postcards and point out all the amazing glamour and glitz and glory that make New York the world's greatest city.

On the New York map I stamped these sites with a red rose from my stamp box. I decided to call them Big Rosys.

That night at dinner I showed my family the plan.

"I'll take Wednesday off," Mom volunteered, "and Dad can take Thursday off, so we can show Duncan those parts of the city you can't get to."

"Even though we've agreed to waitress at our friend Carmen's family restaurant over school vacation, Anitra and I will try to do whatever we can for your tour, Rosy," Pippa offered.

My plan was complete.

When my teacher, Mrs. Oliphant, gave my class an assignment to keep a journal over the vacation week, I bought a special notebook and labeled it "Touring the Town with Duncan." Since it would soon be full of some amazing experiences, I planned to submit it to *The Read-O-Reader*, our school newspaper, for publication.

Every Monday, I sent Duncan a postcard from my postcard book of famous city landmarks, so he would be prepared when he arrived. I mailed them on my way to school after showing them to Hermione and Christy.

"Every tour should have a theme," Christy advised. "My mom does gardens. My dad does Revolutionary battlefields. I do celebrity hangouts. What's your theme?"

"My theme is the 'Only in New York' landmark sites from my collection of postcards," I told Christy.

"Even with a theme, something might happen to mess up your tour," Hermione warned. "There could be bad weather or somebody could catch the flu. You need a backup plan."

And just in case I didn't understand that the backup plan was called Hermione Wong, she went on. "You and Duncan could come along with my family for dim sum in Chinatown."

"Dim sum in Chinatown is not in my postcard book," I told her, "or on my tour."

On my wall calendar I marked the day of Duncan's arrival with a red circle and called it "D Day."

Every night I crossed off the day, watching D Day get closer and closer, until finally I was writing my very last postcard.

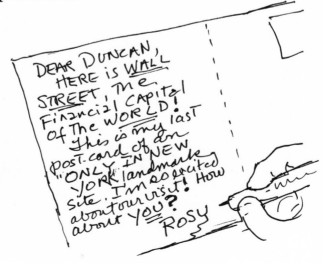

DEAR DUNCAN,
HERE IS WALL
STREET, The
Financial Capital
of The WORLD!
This is my last
post-card of an
"ONLY IN NEW
YORK" landmark
site. I'm so excited
about our visit! How
about YOU?
ROSY

3

On the morning HE was to arrive, Anitra and Pippa slept late. They had worked the dinner shift at Mamacita's restaurant. Mom and Dad slept late, too. They were coming down with colds.

"I feel dreadful," Mom said, breathing in the steam from her hot tea. "I'm afraid I won't be up for much entertaining."

"Me neither," Dad croaked. He popped a zinc lozenge in his mouth and looked at his wristwatch. "But we better get dressed and catch a taxi out to the airport."

·

I was glad I didn't have a cold. First impressions are important. I searched in my costume box for an outfit that would say, "Welcome to New York." But the only thing that fit was left over from Halloween. It would be perfect—if Duncan were arriving by boat instead of flying here.

When Dad announced we had to get going, I had only a minute to throw on my same old clothes that didn't say anything.

We arrived just in time to watch Duncan's plane taxi up to the gate. Out came a woman with three small children and an old man who used a cane and a lady who held a bunch of flowers. Then there was someone who had a sign pinned to his jacket.

The sign said: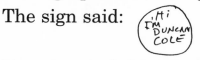

It was a good thing he had on a sign, because even though I had studied his picture a million times, I would never have recognized him.

Sometimes I had pictured Duncan with dark hair and brown eyes or even redheaded with freckles.

But I had never pictured him

waxy white with a barf bucket around his neck. The only good thing about my first impression of Duncan Cole was that the bucket was empty.

"How was your trip?" Mom asked.

"Bumpy. The seat-belt sign was on the whole time." He sighed like an old man. "My mom says, if you want trouble, go travel."

"Your troubles are over," Dad assured him heartily. "In our household, there will be no bumps."

Duncan looked dubious. "My folks

told me you don't have a car either."

"Nobody needs a car in the city," Dad said as we took our place in the taxi line.

In the cab, Dad sat up front with the driver. Duncan and Mom had window seats in the back, with me squashed in between. Ahead of us was a truck belching out black smoke. Behind us was a car with its horn blaring. All around us were dull gray buildings against a dull gray sky. Dad kept looking at the ticking meter. Mom kept blowing her nose. Duncan stared straight ahead.

"Fortunately, it's not that long a trip," Dad told Duncan. That was just before we got stuck in traffic.

"Look, Duncan!" I pointed to the view of the city skyline that suddenly appeared in the window to the west.

Duncan held up his bucket. "Mustn't move my head."

The driver pulled a pine-tree-shaped deodorizer from behind his sunscreen and mumbled something about new seat covers. What was his problem? At least he was sitting up front and would soon see the last of us. I, however, was in for a full week of . . . suddenly I didn't know what.

When we arrived at the apartment, there was a sign on the door. It said: WELCOME DUNCAN.

"You'll be in my room," Pippa told Duncan. "I'll double up with Anitra."

She led him down the hall. "I've cleared out a couple of drawers and a space in the closet. Feel free to make yourself at home."

Duncan glanced around the room, checking out Pippa's guitar and her punk rock posters. He opened his suitcase and removed a shirt, which he draped over a picture of Pippa's favorite group—The Creepy Crawler Band. Then he began to unpack. Along with shirts labeled for all different kinds of weather (HOT/COOL/MUGGY/DAMP), there were underwear labeled for each day of the week and plastic bags of trail mix labeled for every hour of the day.

"My mom said I should avoid strange foods that could be spicy or salty or full of unknown ingredients that could cause choking or hives or low blood sugar," Duncan said as he pulled a list of forbidden foods from his pocket.

In his knapsack there was a germ mask; an antibacterial kit for hands, face, and body; a water bottle with its own filter; a cell phone; a room intercom—and a small leather case, which Duncan pressed to his heart. "But this is what I cannot live without," he said, looking serious.

"A portable air purifier?" I guessed.

With a shy smile, he opened the case and took out a shiny harmonica, which he put in his pocket. "What do we do now?" he asked, looking around the room as if he were lost.

I went to fetch his tour schedule, his map, and his tour kit.

"Big Rosys are all the amazing sites I sent you postcards about," I explained.

Duncan studied the schedule as if it were instructions for an examination. "What about the family party at the end of the week? That wasn't on any postcard."

"The family party is just my mother's family get-together. It's not really a Big Rosy," I said.

"My mom says family is more trouble than it's worth."

"She could have a point," I heard Anitra whisper to Pippa. Then in a loud voice she announced, "Oh, dear, I am *so* sorry, we've got to run. Our friend Carmen asked us to help out at Mamacita's. Two waitresses didn't show. It's an emergency."

An emergency? Didn't they realize that suddenly, without warning, Duncan had become an emergency, too?

In the kitchen Mom and Dad were drinking more hot tea. "Afraid we're not feeling up to the Circle Line boat trip around Manhattan," Mom said after a sneezing fit. "Why don't you two take a walk around the neighborhood instead?"

"There's plenty to see," Dad suggested, handing me an envelope with some bills.

A walk around the neighborhood? Plenty to see? I had planned a cruise around the entire island of Manhattan on which we could view the mansions and high-rises of the rich and famous. The gorgeous penthouses overlooking the East River. The fantastic bridges that link the boroughs of our city and upon which generations of New Yorkers have found poetry and inspiration.

A walk around the neighborhood?

Eddie the doorman? The deli on Madison? The stationery store? The place where my sisters buy blue jeans?

This was not my idea of Day One's Grand Opening Tour.

4

I put on my jacket. Duncan put on his. Even though he had taken off the sign and bucket, I was relieved when the elevator passed Hermione's floor without stopping.

But just when I thought we had an all clear, guess who popped off the lobby bench.

"I'm Rosy's best friend and neighbor, Hermione Wong, wishing you bon voyage on your Circle Line tour."

"We aren't going on the Circle Line," Duncan blabbed. "We're just going for a walk around the neighborhood."

"What a coincidence," Hermione gasped. "Me, too." And before I could stop her, she followed us out the door, down the street, and around the corner toward Central Park, pointing out all the sights along the way. "That's where we buy our fruit and vegetables, and that's where we find the best school supplies, and that's where they sell great home-baked bread."

"I don't think fruit and vegetables and school supplies are why Duncan came all the way to New York," I finally cut in. "They are not exactly tourist sights."

"You mean like the Central Park Zoo?" Hermione seemed to have all the answers. "The little red pandas are my second most favorite endangered species," she gushed, batting her eyelashes at Duncan as if he were the first. "We are halfway there."

It wasn't till we reached the entrance turnstile that I realized something. "I forgot to bring my money."

"Me, too," Duncan cried, feeling in his pockets and looking panicky. "Also my trail mix and my cell phone. I promised my mom I wouldn't go anywhere without them."

"Cheer up." Hermione pointed out the stone fence around the children's zoo. "We can peek over the wall for free and still see something really special."

Duncan gazed over the wall at a few drowsy animals. "Goats and sheep?

What's special about them?" He turned away, disappointed. "In *my* town we have a petting zoo where the sheep are called Daisy and Gus and the goat is Beth. They actually know me and come to greet me when I call them." He closed his eyes for a moment as if he were trying to see them. When he opened his eyes, they looked wet. "What's next?" he whispered, his voice a little wobbly.

"There's always the Metropolitan Museum of Art." I pointed uptown. "If Hermione will treat."

"We have a museum," Duncan said, dragging his feet as if they weighed a ton. "Only it's free. It's got stuff about where we live and all the people we know and who know us and stuff about the families who have lived in my town for hundreds of years."

"The Metropolitan Museum is not about the people you know and where they and their families live—unless you hang out in the Temple of Dendur and have King Tut and Joan of Arc for ancestors." I couldn't believe Duncan

thought his museum at home was anything like the Met. "It's about the
whole world and its art and history."

Suddenly Duncan stopped in his
tracks, staring past me, his eyes
huge with excitement. "Awesome," he
gasped.

Was it the museum? Was it the mansions on Fifth Avenue? What *finally*
impressed him?

He breathed in and leaned forward. "What is that smell?"

Hermione and I looked at each other in disbelief.

"It's just New York pretzels," I said. "Covered with salt and not for free."

Duncan pulled his mother's list of forbidden foods from his pocket. "Covered with salt. I can't eat them," he said. "But a bottle of juice would be okay to prevent low blood sugar." He appealed to Hermione. "Do you have any change? It's an EMERGENCY."

Hermione fished around in her jacket pocket and found a bunch of coins. "We can afford juice and treats *or* the museum," she said. "Not both."

For an answer, Duncan selected an orange drink. He only stopped guzzling it long enough to watch the vendor spread mustard on our pretzels.

"It's a New York thing," I explained.

We took our food to a bench by the lake and watched the ducks circling near the restaurant in the park, waiting for diners to toss them bread.

"We have a lake at home," Duncan told us. "It's so clean you can see the bottom. No garbage. It's got a heron and an osprey on it."

I waited for him to say the heron was called Frances and the osprey Herbert. Was it his zoo against my zoo? His museum against my museum? His lake against my lake?

"This lake," I began slowly, deciding to put something on it that would leave Duncan speechless, "had *our* Great-Grandpa Cole in a rowboat one summer day long ago asking our great-grandma to be his wife."

Duncan *was* speechless all right, but, unfortunately, not Hermione.

"After they decided to get married here," she blurted out, telling a family story I was now sorry I'd ever written up for Family History Week, "they actually lived here."

"*Lived* here? In Central Park?" Duncan's eyes grew huge, and he pressed down on the bench as if he were testing a mattress.

"During the depression people lived in shacks in Central Park. They called the area Hooverville because Hoover was President," Hermione the historian informed us.

"It was only for a few days before some cousins took them in," I added quickly. "They finally found work and made enough money to move to a place of their own." I put down my pretzel. I had lost my appetite.

"My mom says you can't breathe in this town without money. She says people have to live doubled up, all squeezed together like sardines stacked on the shelf, and send their kids out to work in order to make ends meet." Duncan pulled himself to his feet and put his empty soda bottle in the trash. "She says when you travel, you learn that there's no place like home." He pointed to my half pretzel on the bench. "Too salty?"

"Not hungry," I said. "Some birds will eat it."

I went to throw my soda can away. When I looked back, my pretzel was gone.

"Duncan thinks if the birds can eat it and we can eat it, maybe it's okay for him to eat it," Hermione said, explaining my cousin to me.

Duncan nodded. "It's not really *that* salty," he mumbled through stuffed cheeks.

As we walked into the apartment, the phone was ringing. "It's your folks," Dad said, passing the receiver to Duncan. "They say they've been calling you on your cell phone all afternoon."

"I left it in my knapsack by mistake," Duncan explained to his parents. "I didn't need the barf bucket or the intercom, since this entire place could fit in the corner of our kitchen . . . They both have bad colds." He listened for a moment, growing more and more alarmed, then hung up and ran to his room.

"My folks say it's good to be on the safe side," he told us when he returned.

Before I went to bed, I wrote in my journal:

DAY ONE
DOESN'T
COUNT!
Tomorrow will be
The first day of
the FABULOUS
BIG ROSY
TOUR of
NEW YORK.

5

The next morning at breakfast I announced our tour schedule. "Number One, the Empire State Building, where you can enjoy a spectacular view of the entire city of New York. Followed by Number Two, a walk up fabulous Fifth Avenue to—Number Three, legendary Rockefeller Center and a tour of the television studios, where we will join in a live taping of a show."

"Who's driving?" Duncan asked, looking nervous.

"The Fifth Avenue bus to Thirty-fourth Street."

"Dress warmly," Mom advised. She and Dad had fevers and were taking the day off from work.

Duncan showed me an envelope marked $, then he pinned it to his pants. I took my wallet, he loaded up his knapsack, and we were ready to go.

This time we had good luck. Hermione wasn't waiting in the lobby —and a bus was waiting at the stop on Fifth Avenue.

So were a long line of people trying to get on it. "Squeeze in, squeeze in, plenty of room in the back," the driver shouted, though there wasn't any I could see.

As I pushed Duncan ahead of me up the steps, he called over his shoulder, "I forgot to mention, I have a problem with crowds."

After the door closed, the driver

made an announcement. "Due to the President's visit, this bus will detour to the West Side, where connections can be made by subway or bus."

"Oh, good," I told Duncan, pretending I knew about making connections I'd never made before. "This way you'll see even more of my fabulous city."

"Really?" he asked. "How's that?"

When we finally got off on Broadway, I decided to follow the crowd into the downtown subway.

The platform was packed. Only two people were happy about this.

While I was busy trying to listen to the voice on the loudspeaker, Duncan was busy supporting the arts. "How do you get to play down here?" he asked.

SUPPORT
THE
ARTS

"You audition for Music Under New York if you want the best spots," the musician told him just as the train was coming. "There are twenty-three judges, and tryouts are at Grand Central Station, but anybody can play up on the street or in the park. No one will stop you." He looked around hopefully as the doors of the train opened and people poured out. "Some folks who start down here end up on a real stage. You never know who could be in the audience." He struck a chord. "Here they come."

"And here we go." I was only able to coax Duncan into the car because just ahead of us were two men wearing jackets that said "The Harmony Brothers."

"Hello, everyone. We are temporarily unbooked," the brothers announced before breaking into a two-part number. "We'd appreciate anything you can spare."

Duncan dumped all his loose change into the cup. "I am a supporter of the arts," he explained proudly.

At Thirty-fourth Street I was only able to coax him off the train because on the platform he spotted a xylophone player with a tambourine strapped to his foot and a harmonica in a holder around his neck.

"I just got here and I have supported the arts *three* times," Duncan said.

"Keep it up, buddy, and they'll name a concert hall after you," Xyloman told him.

"Save your money," I advised, pulling Duncan up the steps. "We have a full day ahead of us." I pointed out the huge skyscraper down the street.

"I forgot to m-mention," Duncan began to stammer, "I have a little problem with heights." He looked back at the subway longingly.

At the Empire State Building we bought our tickets, went through security, and caught an elevator up to the observation deck on the 102nd floor. "Just imagine, Duncan," I said on the ride up. "This was the tallest building in the whole world until 1973. On a clear day you can see eighty miles and five states. You will look out over Brooklyn, the Bronx, and Staten Island, so get ready for the most spectacular Big Rosy View you've ever seen."

When we arrived at our floor, I gently pulled his cold hands away from his sweaty face and led him onto the observation deck. "Here we are."

He opened one eye and stared into the thick fog. "Where's that?"

I could hardly speak. How could I have been so stupid and not noticed the weather? "The most spectacular view of the entire city you *never* saw," I said, pulling him back into the down elevator before he had a chance to open the other eye.

"Listen, Duncan." I started talking fast. "Forget the view. We will *now* begin our once-in-a-lifetime walk up fabulous Fifth Avenue to legendary Rockefeller Center, where we'll see a live taping of a TV show. Crowded buses, scary heights, and ruined views are in the past. My Big Rosy World-Renowned Rockefeller Center Tour is about to begin."

Down on 34th Street, we headed over to Fifth Avenue—and into the middle of a protest march. "Officer, we have to get through," I pleaded with a cop on a horse.

"Sorry, the President is in town," he yelled down at me. "He's going to speak at the United Nations. We've sealed off the entire route except for security and the press."

"The press," I said, jumping with excitement. "That's me. The *Read-O-Reader*, Star Reporter."

He laughed out loud, and for a moment I thought maybe he'd let us through, but Duncan pulled at my sleeve. "Let's get out of here," he

begged. "I told you I have a problem with crowds."

We had no choice but to go with the crowd right up to Forty-second Street. Then it started to rain.

"I forgot my umbrella," Duncan gasped.

"It's only a few drops," I assured him, rushing over to an umbrella-hat vendor. "Here, put on one of these."

He shook his head. "Back home, if you wore a thing like that, you'd get ribbed so much you'd be better off wet."

"Look around you, Duncan," I said, "and you'll see that when it comes to hats, you're no longer back home."

He gazed at the passing crowd. His cheeks were wet, and it wasn't rain. "You're right," he nodded. "I'm not home and I'm soaked and . . ." His eyes fell on the souvlaki stand next to the

58

hat vendor. "I'm famished and . . ." He felt in all his pockets. "I forgot my trail m-mix again. I bet that food is so spicy and so salty I can't even eat it."

I didn't know if it was his problem with crowds or heights or salt or spices or low blood sugar, but Duncan Cole looked like he was having the worst day of his life.

Just then an ambulance raced by with sirens wailing. I wanted to flag it down like a taxi, shove my cousin inside, and wave goodbye.

Why did my parents have to be sick anyway? Why had I told Hermione and Christy I wouldn't share my tour? And what about Pippa and Anitra, waitressing at Mamacita Mexico for the entire week, just when I needed them?

Mamacita Mexico! I grabbed Duncan by the hand.

"What's up?" he asked.

"We are going to surprise Pippa and Anitra," I told him, heading for the nearest uptown bus. "Let's go eat."

6

LANDMARK
GUACAMOLE

"What are you doing here?" Pippa asked as we came in the door of Mamacita's.

"Guacamole for two," I told her, heading toward a table by the window as if I'd reserved it. The restaurant was warm and dry and cheerful. There were bowls of corn chips and salsa on the white tablecloths. "Charge it to your account," I said. My sisters owed me one.

When the waiter arrived carrying a tray of fresh avocados along with dishes of chopped onion, pepper, cilantro, and herbs to be mixed together into a made-to-order guacamole, Duncan checked his mother's list of forbidden foods. "Do you think it's okay for me to eat this?" he asked.

"What could be wrong with guacamole prepared at the table to your own specifications at a restaurant owned by my sister's friend's father, who learned to cook from his mother in Mexico?" I said. "Just don't eat the salsa. It has hot peppers."

Duncan began to nibble little mouthfuls, but as Carmen's Uncle José and

his mariachi band started to play, the nibbling turned into chewing and then gobbling. "This music carries me away," Duncan said. One thing it carried him away from was his mother's list of forbidden foods. Chomping to the mariachi beat, he ate up every dish in sight, including the salsa with hot peppers.

"That concertina sounds just like a harmonica," Duncan exclaimed at the break, pointing out Carmen's cousin Manuel, who plays and sings with the band on school holidays and weekends. "Is he our age?"

"All the family are in the band," I admitted, waiting for Duncan to tell me his mother was right about New York children having to work to make ends meet.

Instead, he leaped up from his chair. "I forgot to wash," he said, grabbing his notebook and running off to find the bathroom.

After a while Pippa came by our table to take away the empty plates. "Any dessert?" she asked. "Given that I seem to be paying?"

"Duncan's been washing his hands for ten minutes," I said.

Pippa shook her head. "He's showing Manuel his harmonica and taking notes. Maybe he wants a job."

When Duncan finally came back, he looked excited. "I played for Manuel, and he says I'm pretty good. He started to teach me 'Guantanamera,' and he's going to call to make a date to teach me 'Cielito Lindo.'"

After lunch we walked to the cross-town bus stop. Since Anitra had made me a rain scarf out of a delivery bag, I let Duncan borrow my hat.

When the bus driver announced, "Due to continued flooding, this bus will have to detour," I was not surprised.

Someone laughed and then someone groaned, and a woman next to me burst out crying. "Today is my birth-day," she whimpered. "I just broke up

with my boyfriend and my family is two thousand miles away and they are going to call ten minutes from now and I won't be home in time."

Nobody said a word, and then an old man began to sing in a high croaking voice. "Happy birthday to you." It didn't take long before more and more people joined in, so that by the time we got through to the other side of the park everybody on the bus was singing "Happy Birthday," and the woman was laughing and waving thank you.

When we climbed down from the bus, Duncan said, "My mom told me not to talk to strangers, but that doesn't mean I can't *sing* with them—or play the harmonica for them either." His face broke into a grin and he played a chord. "So where to next, Rosy?" he asked.

I was so exhausted I could hardly move. "Home," I said. "Maybe I'll think of something."

My parents had left a note stuck to the front door.

I nearly wept with joy. "It's not on our schedule, Duncan," I said, "but the next Big Rosy of the day is A NAP."

When I woke up, the phone was ringing. It was Christy. "How'd the tour go?" she asked.

"I took your advice about finding a theme," I said. "My theme is Rosy Cole's Worst Ever, Totally Terrible, Get-Stuck-in-Traffic-and-Never-See-Anything Tour of the Town."

"Why don't you call Hermione. I'm sure she'd love to help out."

I was sure, too.

"We're very busy this week," Hermione said when I asked her to share in my tour. "Tomorrow my mom is taking me to Wall Street to see the Stock Exchange and to South Street Seaport to see the tall ships." She sighed as if she were doing me a big favor. Which she was. "We'll meet you in the lobby at ten. I hope you won't forget that's what friends are for."

I wouldn't forget because she would never let me.

In my journal I wrote,

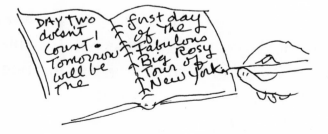

DAY TWO
doesn't
count!
Tomorrow
will be
the

first day
of the
fabulous
Big Rosy
Tour of
New York.

7

"But I want to make a rehearsal date with Manuel," Duncan complained when I announced the plan for the day. "I told you he said I could go over to his place so he could teach me some of his songs."

A rehearsal date? Manuel? "Tell Manuel your rehearsal will have to wait."

So Duncan called Manuel. "Guess what?" he reported back. "Today Manuel promised to help his cousin Hector, who works on Wall Street. Maybe we'll see him there."

70

"Maybe we'll see him there?" I wanted to laugh. "You've got to be kidding. Wall Street and the New York Stock Exchange are the financial center of the whole world, Duncan," I said, showing him a postcard photo of the jam-packed trading floor. "What goes on at the New York Stock Exchange will affect people ALL OVER THE GLOBE."

"Why are you yelling?" he asked.

"Because Wall Street is not like a small town where you run into people you know."

Duncan packed his knapsack. He took money, trail mix, hand sanitizer, filtered water bottle, notebook, and harmonica. The list of forbidden foods was in his pocket. But he left his cell phone under the bed.

Just as we were leaving, Anitra called out to say goodbye. "Since Mom is still sick, I'll take you both on the ferry to Ellis Island tomorrow," she said.

I hugged her and thanked her. "Now I owe *you* one," I whispered. Was my luck about to turn?

Hermione and Mrs. Wong were waiting for us in the lobby. There was no crowd on the subway platform. The train came right away and it was nearly empty. My luck was changing for sure.

"I have some errands to do in Chinatown before we go on our tour," Mrs. Wong announced. "This is our stop."

She led us up the subway stairs onto one of the narrow streets of Chinatown. It was crammed with markets selling all kinds of food. Mrs. Wong inspected fish in ice-packed trays out on the sidewalk. At the vegetable stand she felt each item before she bought it. "Just look how beautiful," she said, holding up a bunch of fresh litchis before placing them on the scale. She showed us how to peel back the pink skin and suck the soft white fruit out with all its sweet juice.

"Much better than the dried ones."

The litchis were delicious, but they weren't Wall Street or the New York Stock Exchange or South Street Seaport. They weren't one of my Big Rosys and it was getting late. How long would shopping take?

Hermione began to point and jump. "There's Auntie Jen," she said, waving to a woman who was selecting a Chinese cabbage.

Soon Mrs. Wong was hugging and kissing Auntie Jen, and Auntie Jen was inviting us to her restaurant for lunch.

"Auntie Jen's restaurant is only a few minutes' walk from here," Mrs. Wong said. "There's nothing better to eat on a chilly day than her Mongolian hot pot."

"Some members of our family have lived here in Chinatown for years," Hermione boasted. "They could really show Duncan around."

What was going on? All of a sudden we were on the Big Hermione Tour.

"Actually," I said, catching sight of a familiar street sign, "this wasn't always part of Chinatown. Our Grandma Cole's father grew up in one of the buildings on that street." I pointed out a row of old tenement houses.

"He did?" Duncan was completely amazed.

"That's right," Hermione chimed in. "His parents were the janitors of the building." Before I could stop her, she launched into the rest of my Family History Week essay. "They lived in four rooms with eight kids and slept three to a bed. The toilets were out back. There was no heat and no hot running water. In summer they swam in the water tank on the roof to cool off, until they were caught."

"But that was before Great-Grandpa went to work as a trolley conductor and saved up for engineering school and moved uptown to a big apartment," I said. "End of story."

But it wasn't. "Your great-*grandma's* poppa was a peddler who sold fruit and veggies from a cart," Hermione went on. I couldn't believe how she had committed to memory my entire family essay. There was no stopping her.

"When he came from Russia by himself at thirteen, right away he said, 'New York is my home.' He even sold his train ticket to Chicago and moved in with an aunt and uncle. He lived with them until he had saved enough money to buy his own grocery store," she concluded, beaming at me as if she'd just won first prize in a memory contest.

When we got to the restaurant, there was a big fish tank full of live fish that would be cooked up when customers ordered them. Auntie Jen told the waiter to bring us a bubbling basin of broth and place it on a burner in the middle of the round table. There were plates of uncooked fish and meat. We all had our own little metal basket to use to submerge the raw food into the broth until it was cooked.

Duncan took his bag of trail mix out of his pocket and put it on the table. "I'm not sure I should eat such strange food," he explained, eyeing the uncooked fish and meat.

"Strange?" Mrs. Wong repeated. "You cook it yourself. How can that be strange? It's a New York soup. All different kinds of things go into the pot to make the richest, healthiest broth in the world. When we're done, I take the leftover broth home to my freezer."

Duncan squirted sanitizer on his palms before carefully loading his basket and lowering it into the simmering broth. We all watched him take his first sip.

"Could I take some broth home, too?" he asked.

"We need another order," Mrs. Wong told Auntie Jen.

I looked at my watch. Mongolian hot pot was delicious, but it was NOT a Big Rosy.

When the second order of hot pot was finally finished, we had fruit with fortune cookies.

Hermione and Duncan got the same message: "You will befriend a mysterious stranger."

Before we left the restaurant, Duncan placed the container of broth in his knapsack. He left his trail mix on the table. "For the fish," he said.

At last we were headed down to Wall Street and the Stock Exchange.

"Manuel's helping his cousin Hector, who works on Wall Street," Duncan said. "Maybe we'll see him."

Mrs. Wong seemed doubtful. "Even though it's just one street, thousands of people work on it."

But sure enough, as we came out of the subway, Duncan began to wave and holler. "There he is, Manuel and his cousin Hector."

"Business is not so good today," Hector complained. "Usually I am almost sold out by now. How can I make enough money to open my own restaurant with days like this?"

"You need a mariachi band to attract business," Manuel advised.

"Nothing could help today," Hector said.

" 'Guantanamera'?"

The next thing I knew, Duncan had taken his harmonica out of his pocket and begun to accompany Manuel's singing. Hermione got into the act, snapping her fingers as if they were castanets.

81

Three people paused to listen. Two of them came over to watch, and one of them ordered a taco.

"Maybe you *are* good for business," Hector said.

Mrs. Wong looked at her watch. "If we want to catch the tour of the trading floor at the Stock Exchange, we have to say goodbye."

"Can't we stay here?" Duncan asked.

"Don't you want to watch the biggest stock market in the world in action and learn how money is made?" I cried.

"If we stay right here, we can see for ourselves how money is made," Duncan pointed out.

"Who knows," Hector said. "Maybe my restaurant will become such a success I will open more all over the country and then sell shares on the trading floor, too."

Just then a crammed double-decker bus full of sightseers turned down the narrow street.

" 'Guantanamera' again," Manuel suggested to Duncan.

Someone with a megaphone was shouting to look at this and that. Suddenly I wished we were on it.

"It looks like the trading floor and the tall ships will have to wait till tomorrow, Rosy," Mrs. Wong said.

Duncan stopped playing. "Tomorrow Anitra takes us on a ferry to Ellis Island."

"A ferry to Ellis Island?" I began to laugh. I laughed so hard I couldn't catch my breath.

"What is it, Rosy?" Mrs. Wong asked.

How could I tell her? What would prevent our ferry from landing? An iceberg? Or maybe pirates? How about a tidal wave? The only thing I could be sure of on Rosy Cole's Worst Ever, Totally Terrible Tour of the City of New York was that something would go wrong.

8

What went wrong with our trip to
Ellis Island? Well, before we went to
catch the ferry, we stopped at Manuel's
apartment so his visiting cousin Carmen could teach Anitra a few of the
songs the band performs.

"This won't take long," Anitra assured us. "Even though my instrument
is drums, I'm really getting the hang
of the trumpet, and I love it. Carmen
doesn't have much time for me, so I
have to grab the chance."

Manuel opened the door. While Anitra and Carmen practiced, he showed

us the apartment. It was a long hall with bedrooms off it. There were three or four beds in each small room. "We used to live with two other families when we first came here," Manuel said. "We played on the subway and in the street. But now we have gigs at weddings and birthday parties, and we have two restaurants and an apartment all our own." He showed Duncan his guitar. Duncan took out his harmonica, and before I knew it, Manuel was teaching him how to play a new song. I put cotton in my ears and read a magazine.

I fell asleep in spite of the noise, and when I woke up, Anitra said it was too late to go to Ellis Island. "Maybe some other day."

"He's only here for a week," I reminded her.

"See you tomorrow," Manuel said to Duncan. "Don't forget your knapsack." As he handed it to Duncan, the top flap opened and everything fell out on the floor.

"Why do you carry all this stuff?" Manuel asked, helping to pick everything up.

"My mom told me bad things could happen here," Duncan said.

"That's true," Carmen agreed. "But something bad can happen anywhere.

In our small village in Mexico, bad things were happening to us because of our politics and our opinions and our thoughts. We came here with nothing but music, recipes, and dreams." She looked around the room with pride. "For some of us New Yorkers, really *good* things happen here."

On the street, Duncan took off his knapsack and carried it in his arms. "I don't want this stuff anymore," he confided. "Maybe I could peddle it like Great-Great-Grandpa."

"Peddle it like Great-Great-Grandpa?" I took his arm so he would listen to me. "*Our* New York is not sleeping three to a bed or swimming in the water tank or *peddling on the street*."

From halfway down the block, I heard Hermione yelling. "Want to buy something?" She had spread a blanket full of her old stuff right beside the entrance to our building.

"There are really good bargains here," Eddie the doorman announced, searching the blanket for something to prove it.

"Could I sell from your blanket, too?" Duncan asked Hermione.

When she said yes, he opened his knapsack and arranged his hand sanitizer, germ mask, antibacterial kit, and trail mix in the middle of her heap. "I'll be right back," he told us, and ran into the building.

Hermione made more room on the blanket, which was a good idea since when Duncan returned he was carrying more things to sell.

Mrs. Raposo our neighbor took the intercom and the antibacterial kit. The remaining trail mix went to Eddie the doorman, and someone actually bought the barf bucket. "For feeling a little sick in the car," the woman said.

I was feeling a little sick myself. Also, I was cold. "I'm going upstairs," I told Duncan.

"I'll be up in a while," he said, smiling at Hermione. "If I play my harmonica, it could be good for your business."

"Thanks, Duncan," she gushed, and then squinted at the sky. "But it looks like it's going to snow."

That night I didn't write in my journal. Instead, I put it away . . . for good.

When I woke up the next morning, a blizzard had turned the sidewalks white—and I had an infection that turned my sore throat white, too.

"You will stay in bed today," my mother ordered after calling the doctor. She gave me a pill and I dozed off.

When I woke up, the phone was ringing.

It was Hermione. "Can you and Duncan come for dinner?" she asked. "My mom is doing a Cantonese feast."

"I'm sick," I said.

"But Duncan isn't."

"It's a blizzard." Duncan pointed out the window. "How will I get there?"

"On the elevator," I croaked, thinking, poor Duncan. Since I was sick, he had no plan for the day. No Big Rosy to look forward to. Nothing to do until dinnertime.

I went back to sleep until Christy phoned a few minutes later with an idea for a snow date in the park with Kiesha and Debby and Donald.

"I'm sick," I said.

"But Duncan isn't."

Before I was halfway through giving

Duncan the message, he was halfway out the door. "Tell her I'll be there in a sec," he crowed. "I'll just take the elevator."

I went back to sleep. Much later I heard Duncan come in. He spoke to me from the door. "We built a fort, and someone named Debby shoved snow down my neck and said she was sorry and invited me to her house to dry off. She invited everyone for hot cocoa, so I thought it would be okay and I went and she lives in this amazing building with a terrace and plants." He seemed to run out of steam, so he just smiled and played me a few chords on his harmonica.

The phone rang. I knew my friends were calling to see how I felt.

Pippa poked her head in the door.

"It's for you, Duncan," she said.

Duncan grabbed the phone from her hand and listened. "Manuel wants to know if I can come to his place. Don't worry. I remember where it is."

The next time I woke up, Duncan was returning from Manuel's. "I met the whole family and helped them shovel snow off the stoop. Manuel showed me some more chords on the guitar and taught me 'Cielito Lindo' in Spanish. I learned the words and played along on my harmonica."

I had broth for dinner and a piece of dry toast. I must have dozed off because the next time I saw Duncan he had just come back from a Cantonese feast at Hermione's.

"And best of all, I've been working on a new song, Rosy," he said, settling down on the end of my bed. "It's called 'New York Hot Pot' and it's dedicated to you."

"New York Hot Pot"! Instead of devoting a song to the Empire State Building, the Stock Exchange, the Statue of Liberty, or Ellis Island, Duncan was writing a song about a hot pot. My Big Rosy Tour was truly pathetic.

Tomorrow was Friday and Duncan was going home on Sunday. I hardly had any time left. I was desperate for a great idea. An inspiration. Maybe it was the fever, but suddenly I got one. I would talk to Dad about it in the morning.

I fell asleep, happy at last.

Tomorrow would be the first day of the . . .

FABULOUS ROSY COLE TOUR OF THE . . . . .

97

10

"Lunch at the Plaza Hotel?" Dad yelped the next morning when he heard my plan. Then I reminded him that because of his cold and Mom's cold and Anitra's and Pippa's waitressing and my being sick and the President's being in New York and flooding on the crosstown bus route and fog and snow and rain, Duncan hadn't seen one real Big Rosy.

"Okay, okay," he said, reaching for his wallet and counting out enough for the cheapest item on the menu. "But don't go overboard."

I told Duncan to put on his blazer and his flannel pants. I dressed in my Dream Teen Silk Extravaganza. I had never in my life been to the Plaza Hotel.

"Do we have to go?" Duncan asked as we were about to leave.

"You've been a tourist for almost a week, and you haven't seen any of the New York places I planned for us to see."

"But you can see them all the time, and I'm not interested."

"Me? I've never seen any of them!"

"What?" He was astonished. "They're *your* Big Rosys."

"In case you haven't noticed, I am not a tourist," I said. "I live here. Real New Yorkers don't have to check out the monuments and buildings to know how it feels to belong here."

The lobby of the Plaza was all gilt and marble and uniforms, glitz and glitter. It was my dream come true. At last Duncan would experience a Big Rosy. "Keep your eyes open, Duncan," I advised. "This is where the elite meet. Wall-to-wall celebrities. The rich and famous at play. When you go home and tell your friends who you spotted, they will turn green with envy."

A waiter led us into the Palm Court. He pulled out a chair for me and then a chair for Duncan. He gave us each a menu.

At last we had arrived. "Dunky Cole," somebody hollered from across the room, "what are YOOOOU doing here?"

"Mrs. Loomis?" Duncan turned pale.

A woman in a tan pantsuit and running shoes raced up to our table and grabbed Duncan in a big hug. She turned to me. "I live just three houses down from Little Dunky, and I've known him since forever." She waved to her table of friends, who all yelled, "Hellloooo."

"Our Theater Club is here for our annual Theater Week. Five shows in five days, and on top of it we see Dunky Cole. Just wait till I tell your folks."

After she headed back to her group, Duncan frowned and looked at his watch. "How long do we have to stay?" he asked. "I'm meeting Manuel. He's going to take me shopping and teach me more songs."

"But I thought we'd take a carriage ride through the park after lunch," I pleaded.

"A carriage ride through the park?" he said with disgust. "You must think I'm some kind of tourist."

So after a lunch that was even

cheaper than Dad had hoped, I walked him up to Manuel's place and left him there.

He didn't get home till nearly dinnertime.

"What's in the big box?" I asked.

"A surprise," Duncan answered. Then he closed his eyes and played "Guantanamera" on the harmonica very softly. We all applauded.

"Will you play for the family party tomorrow?" I asked.

"It will be my first gig," Duncan told me proudly.

The next morning my mother gave us her list of food to pick up at the deli. She and Dad were busy setting up for the family party.

While I stood in line with my mother's list of cold cuts and smoked fish and cheese, Duncan walked off.

When I was done, it wasn't hard to find him.

"I wonder if I could stay a little longer?" Duncan asked. "Olga says she's going to make pierogi. I already tried the tricolor pasta and some of the goat cheeses."

"The family is arriving soon."

"You know what my mom says, 'Family is more trouble than it's worth.'"

"Not ours," I said, realizing that even though they weren't a Big Rosy, my family would not let me down. "When we get together, we have the most fun in the world."

"You mean like friends?"

"I mean like people you know your whole life whose parents and grandparents knew your parents and grandparents."

"I have to go now, Olga," Duncan told the lady at the demonstration. "I won't be able to sample the pierogi."

"Don't worry about it," she said, handing him a sheet of paper. "Here's a list of the stores where I'll be cooking for the rest of the week. You can stop by any of them and I'll give you a taste."

Duncan tucked the list in his pocket, then pulled out his mother's list of forbidden foods and tossed it in the pail of used paper plates. "I'll be there," he said, and waved goodbye.

As soon as we got home, the doorbell started ringing. Everybody was kissing and hugging and hollering "hello."

"So what have you been doing on your visit to New York?" my cousin Mike asked Duncan.

"Rosy's been taking me around," he said. "She made a schedule and gave me a kit." Duncan showed him my Big Rosy Tour box.

All the cousins gathered around for a look. Little Harry grabbed the box. Mike pulled it away.

"No fair," Harry squawked. Mike held the box out of reach, and everything spilled out on the floor.

Harry snatched up the water bottle and took care of Mike.

This was followed by Mike taking care of Harry.

"Are they having the most fun in the world yet?" Duncan asked me.

All of a sudden I couldn't speak. The family party was just like my Fabulous Big Rosy Tour of New York. A bust.

"Hey, Rosy." Mike stopped dealing with Harry. "What's up?"

"Everything," I sobbed. "My family is as big a flop as my tour."

Just like that, Harry gave the water bottle to Mike, who handed him the apple. Mike took a large handkerchief from his pocket and mopped the water off Harry's face. When he was done, he gave Harry the handkerchief and took out three coins. "Help me with a magic trick, Harry?" he asked.

Harry held the handkerchief over the coins, which Mike made disappear, only to pull them from behind Harry's ear.

We all applauded, and Mike took a bow. "A few minutes ago I wanted to make *you* disappear, Harry, but I'm glad I didn't. You're a good assistant," Mike said.

I knew they were all just trying to cheer me up by pretending to be friends, so I decided to pretend to be having a good time.

And looking at Duncan, I could see he was good at pretending, too.

After lunch Aunt Teddy sat down at the piano. "Come on, Rosy, give us a great big smile," she cried. Soon we were all singing. I was so busy following the music I didn't notice that Duncan had slipped out of the room, until he suddenly returned.

"*Buenos días*," he greeted us, tipping what had been the surprise in the box, blowing a chord on the harmonica, and bowing.

"Now I will sing an original song dedicated to my great-great-grandpa and my cousin Rosy, called 'New York Hot Pot.'"

Duncan closed his eyes and in a soft voice began to sing:

All kinds of fish
from all kinds of seas
in a broth so rich
it's bound to please —
Strange food... good food
Hot Pot New York —
Throw in some people
who play different songs
They'll bring their own spices
we'll all get along —
Strange food... good food
Hot Pot New York —
So call up your friends
Make your burner glow bright
bad weather won't stop us
we're eating Hot Pot Tonight!

When he was done, Aunt Teddy hugged him. We all clapped our hands.

"I wish Grandpa were alive to hear you," Mom said. "He never learned to read notes but could play anything the crowd could hum at a dive called the Bowery Rose. Customers would fill his cap with enough money to help pay the rent."

"The Bowery Rose," Uncle Ralph remembered. "It's still there, only now it's a stand-up comedy club with an open-mike night."

For an encore Duncan sang and played "Guantanamera" and ended up joining Aunt Teddy on piano for "East Side, West Side."

Soon my relatives began to look at their watches. "Time to go," they said, searching among the pile of coats on the bed, hugging, kissing, and telling Duncan, "Come back soon" and "Have a good trip."

Now here I was, sitting on my bed with my mother and father and Pippa and Anitra and with two policemen, Officers Fernando and Rogers, standing around me reading Duncan's note and trying to find a clue.

"You must have shown your cousin some amazing sights to make him want to stay on," Officer Rogers said.

"Amazing sights?" I shook my head. "Not one."

Officer Fernando reread Duncan's note. "Too many things I never got to do," he quoted Duncan.

"That's right!" I agreed. "He never got to see any of the postcard sights I promised."

"Let's take a look at those post-cards," Officer Rogers suggested. "They could be a clue to where we'll find him."

Officer Fernando called headquarters and sent out an all points bulletin to every tourist location on my list. Pippa went to make copies of Duncan's photo from the Christmas card so she could post them all over the neighborhood.

Dad called Uncle Grover. "Hi, Grover," he said in a booming voice. "It turns out there were a few more things Duncan just had to see before flying home, so he'll take a flight sometime tomorrow. No need to worry."

"*I* am worried sick," Mom said. None

of us could eat a thing all day. We stared at the phone, and we looked out the window, watching the sun begin to sink over the park as the sky darkened. We were all thinking that Duncan was somewhere out there. But where?

"He signs himself 'Real New Yorker,' " Dad said. "Is that a clue?"

Pippa and Anitra had to go to Mamacita's. They didn't want to leave us. It had begun to rain. They put on their coats. I walked them to the door and waited with them for the elevator, watching the numbers that told you the car was coming and praying Duncan would miraculously be in it.

And then suddenly . . .

He was.

"Where were you?" he wailed. "You never came to find me like cousins do. I waited all day."

"We've been worried sick," Mom said, grabbing Duncan and giving him a hug. "We called the police and waited by the phone while they checked out the tourist spots Rosy never got to show you."

SUPPORT THE ARTS

"Tourist spots?" Duncan burst out. "I'm not interested in tourist spots! I sang on the street just like Great-Grandpa. I played for Hector's taco stand. I checked out the Comedy Club. I went to eat Olga's pierogi. TOURIST SPOTS?" he repeated with disgust.

At Mamacita's, where we all went to celebrate Duncan's return/farewell—in a sendoff dinner—he waved at Manuel. "There are still so many things I never got to do," he said sadly. "I never got to audition for Music Under New York or practice with Manuel for our own group or go to Hermione's birthday party."

"You never got to go home either," Mom said.

"But I am home," Duncan told her. "I'm a real New Yorker. Like Rosy said, real New Yorkers don't have to check out the monuments and buildings to know how it feels to belong here."

"But if you know how it feels, you can take the feeling with you anywhere you go, no matter what," Dad said.

"Until you come back," Mom added.

The next day, watching Duncan board his plane, we waved and blew kisses. "He looks different," Dad observed, putting his arm around my shoulder. "In spite of what you think, Rosy, that tour you planned for Duncan Cole changed his life."

I didn't say anything.

We both knew it wasn't the tour I *planned* that changed Duncan's life. It was another tour. One you couldn't put

in a picture, or point out from a sight-seeing bus or the deck of the Circle Line. It was a tour of all the reasons New Yorkers who love our city call it home . . .

The Worst Ever, Best Yet Little Rosy Tour—that I never even knew I gave.

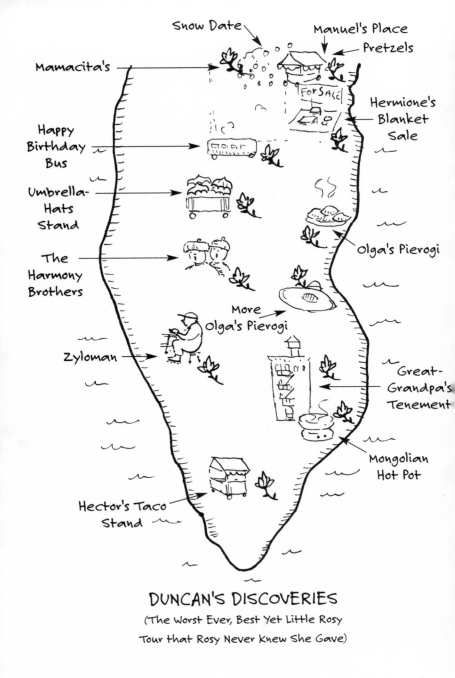

Snow Date

Manuel's Place
Pretzels

Mamacita's

Hermione's
Blanket
Sale

Happy
Birthday
Bus

Umbrella-
Hats
Stand

Olga's Pierogi

The
Harmony
Brothers

More
Olga's Pierogi

Zyloman

Great-
Grandpa's
Tenement

Mongolian
Hot Pot

Hector's Taco
Stand

DUNCAN'S DISCOVERIES
(The Worst Ever, Best Yet Little Rosy
Tour that Rosy Never knew She Gave)